DreamWorks

DRAGONS

THOR
BONECRUSHER

HODDER CHILDREN'S BOOKS

First published by Nelson Verlag, Völckersstraße 14–20, 22765 Hamburg

First published in Great Britain in 2018 by Hodder and Stoughton

ISBN: 978 1 444 94451 8

Printed and bound in China by RR Donnelley Asia Printing Solutions Limited

The paper and board used in this book are made from wood from responsible sources

FSC
www.fsc.org

MIX
Paper from
responsible sources
FSC® C104740

Hodder Children's Books
An imprint of
Hachette Children's Group
Part of Hodder and Stoughton
Carmelite House
50 Victoria Embankment
London, EC4Y 0DZ

An Hachette UK Company
www.hachette.co.uk

www.hachettechildrens.co.uk

The Dragon Riders were looking for a Scauldron dragon who had eaten all the fish around Berk. They had waited for a long time. But when the Scauldron finally appeared, Fishlegs sneezed so loudly that the dragon took off.

"What's up with Fishlegs?" Astrid asked. Her friend's nose was running, he was constantly sneezing and scratching his face as if he had fallen into an anthill.

"Hmmm ..." Hiccup said. "This always happens when you ride Meatlug. Fishlegs, I think you are allergic to your dragon!"

"No, that can't be!" Fishlegs sniffed. But the other Dragon Riders were sure. He had a Meatlug allergy and there was only one person that could help: old Gothi.

Gothi was the healer of Berk. She looked at her new patient very carefully. Then she swung her stick in front of his nose and immediately Fishlegs began to snore.

"Is he hypnotised now?" asked Snotlout in a whisper.

"You are NOT allergic to Meatlug," Hiccup said several times, trying to charm his friend into believing it.

Snotlout had another idea though. He rushed to the snoring Fishlegs and shouted: "You are a mighty, fearless Viking!"

"Fishlegs?" Hiccup asked, as his friend opened his eyes.

"Who is Fishlegs?" snorted Fishlegs. "My name is Thor. Thor Bonecrusher!" He grabbed Gothi's stick and broke it in two.

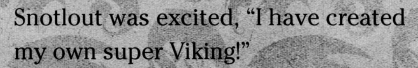

Snotlout was excited, "I have created my own super Viking!"

The villagers were confused.

"I need a worthy weapon," Fishlegs told Gobber the village blacksmith as he grabbed an axe.

"But that's Stoick's battle axe!" Gobber cried.

"Pah!" snarled Fishlegs, "if he wants it, he can try to take it away from me!"

"We're going to get that Scauldron!"
Fishlegs shouted, dragging Snotlout to
his dragon.

The two jumped on Hookfang and
flew out to sea, right into the middle
of a storm.

"Thor Bonecrusher will conquer the beast!" Fishlegs roared as the Scauldron appeared.

Meanwhile, the others thought about how to get their old friend back.

Gothi thought shocking him could help but to do that they would need to bring him back to Berk.

As the friends made a plan to rescue
Fishlegs a storm began far out over
the sea. They could not wait any longer
so the Dragon Riders flew off.

"There he is!" Astrid shouted. Fishlegs had jumped onto the Scauldron's back and was trying to tame him.

Hiccup did not know what to do and
was about to turn back when Meatlug
appeared next to him out of nowhere.

She had followed the Dragon Riders
and was flying directly towards
the Scauldron.

The Scauldron watched the cheeky
Gronckle as smoke rose from his mouth.

That's when Fishlegs froze. "No, not my Meatlug! Leave my dragon alone!" He ran across the back of the Scauldron and jumped onto Meatlug.

Now was the other Dragon Riders'
chance. The twins and Astrid trapped
the Scauldron in a net. They had caught
the dangerous dragon!

The seas around Berk were safe
once again.

Soon Fishlegs was back to his old self.
He was not even sneezing and the itching
had gone too.

Hiccup figured out the real problem.
"Gobber used earwax to polish
Meatlug's saddle, that's what you were
allergic to – not Meatlug!"